Dear Parents:

Congratulations! Your child is taking the first steps on an exciting journey. The destination? Independent reading!

STEP INTO READING® will help your child get there. The program offers five steps to reading success. Each step includes fun stories and colorful art or photographs. In addition to original fiction and books with favorite characters, there are Step into Reading Non-Fiction Readers, Phonics Readers and Boxed Sets, Sticker Readers, and Comic Readers—a complete literacy program with something to interest every child.

Learning to Read, Step by Step!

Ready to Read   Preschool–Kindergarten
• big type and easy words • rhyme and rhythm • picture clues
For children who know the alphabet and are eager to begin reading.

Reading with Help   Preschool–Grade 1
• basic vocabulary • short sentences • simple stories
For children who recognize familiar words and sound out new words with help.

Reading on Your Own   Grades 1–3
• engaging characters • easy-to-follow plots • popular topics
For children who are ready to read on their own.

Reading Paragraphs   Grades 2–3
• challenging vocabulary • short paragraphs • exciting stories
For newly independent readers who read simple sentences with confidence.

Ready for Chapters   Grades 2–4
• chapters • longer paragraphs • full-color art
For children who want to take the plunge into chapter books but still like colorful pictures.

STEP INTO READING® is designed to give every child a successful reading experience. The grade levels are only guides; children will progress through the steps at their own speed, developing confidence in their reading.

Remember, a lifetime love of reading starts with a single step!

Copyright © 2014 Disney Enterprises, Inc. All rights reserved. Pixar characters and artwork copyright © 2014 Disney•Pixar. All rights reserved. Published in the United States by Random House Children's Books, a division of Random House LLC, 1745 Broadway, New York, NY 10019, and in Canada by Random House of Canada Limited, Toronto, Penguin Random House Companies, in conjunction with Disney Enterprises, Inc.

Step into Reading, Random House, and the Random House colophon are registered trademarks of Random House LLC.

Visit us on the Web!
StepIntoReading.com
randomhouse.com/kids

Educators and librarians, for a variety of teaching tools, visit us at RHTeachersLibrarians.com

ISBN 978-0-7364-3270-2 (trade) — ISBN 978-0-7364-8165-6 (lib. bdg.) — ISBN 978-0-7364-3272-6 (ebook)

Printed in the United States of America   10 9 8 7 6 5 4 3 2 1

Random House Children's Books supports the First Amendment and celebrates the right to read.

DISNEY INFINITY

TOY BOX HEROES

By Christy Webster

Illustrated by the Disney Storybook Art Team

Random House 🏠 New York

In the world
of Disney Infinity,
there are many heroes.
Every character
is ready
for an adventure.

In the Play Sets,

there are

missions to complete

and objects to collect.

The Incredibles
use superpowers
to defend their city
from the bad guy
Syndrome.

Captain Jack Sparrow
takes his ship
on the high seas.

Sulley and Mike study

and scare

at Monsters University.

They play pranks

on Fear Tech students.

Every Play Set is
full of adventures.
But in the Toy Box,
there are infinite possibilities!

Anna is brave
and loves having fun.
She likes to climb
and explore.

Wreck-It Ralph
is good at wrecking,
but he wants to be
a good guy.

He cannot jump high,
but he can climb high.

In the Toy Box,
Anna and Ralph can build
frozen mountains
and explore them together.

Friends can join them,
even in the sky!

Mike and Sulley are students
at Monsters University.
Sulley can scare anyone
with a roar.

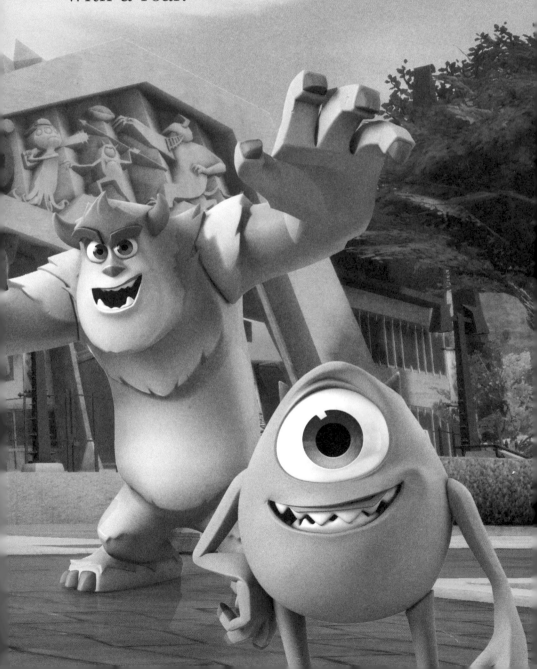

Jessie is a cowgirl doll.

She loves playing.

She can yodel
and wrestle.

Jessie, Mike, and Sulley
can build a town
in the Toy Box.

Then they can work together
to beat the bad guys.

Vanellope races cars
in an arcade game
called *Sugar Rush*.

Lightning McQueen races
around the world.
He has won
four Piston Cups!

In the Disney Infinity Toy Box,
Vanellope and Lightning
can build their own
track and race everyone!

Violet is a young superhero.
She can create
a force field.

Violet uses her power
to protect her friends
from bad guys.

Mater is a rusty

tow truck

from Radiator Springs.

In the Toy Box,

Mater can be

a monster truck

and the star of the show!

Jack Sparrow builds
a pirate village.

His superhero
and monster friends
help him find gold.

Sulley builds

a fairy-tale forest.

He can go on a quest there

with a princess

and a cowgirl.

Anything can happen
in the Toy Box!
What adventures will
the heroes have next?